Ling-Li and the Phoenix Fairy

A CHINESE FOLKTALE

Retold by Ellin Greene

Illustrated by Zong-Zhou Wang

CLARION BOOKS/NEW YORK

Clarion Books
a Houghton Mifflin Company imprint
215 Park Avenue South, New York, NY 10003
Text copyright © 1996 by Ellin Greene
Illustrations copyright © 1996 by Zong-Zhou Wang

The illustrations for this book were executed in acrylics.
The text is set in 15/19-point Centaur.

Retold from *Folk Tales from China*
(Foreign Languages Press, Peking, 1960).

Printed in Singapore

Library of Congress Cataloging-in-Publication Data
Greene, Ellin.
    Ling-Li and the Phoenix Fairy: A Chinese Folktale /
retold by Ellin Greene; illustrated by Zong-Zhou Wang.
        p.   cm.
    "Retold from Folk tales from China (Foreign Languages Press,
Peking)"—T.p. verso.
    Summary: Retells a Chinese tale in which a girl's colorful
wedding robe is stolen and torn into pieces, which ultimately
become the flowers we know as jewelweed.
    ISBN 0-395-71528-8
    [1. Jewelweed—Folklore. 2. Folklore—China.]
I. Wang, Zong-Zhou, 1946– ill. II. Folk tales from China.   III. Title.
PZ8.1.G785Jac   1996
398.2'09510242—dc20
[E]
                                    94-19724
                                       CIP
                                       AC

TWP   10 9 8 7 6 5 4 3 2 1

To Ted and Nancy

"May you live in harmony and have a rich, full life together"

—E.G.

To Earl B. Lewis

—Z.Z.W.

ONCE, LONG AGO, in a small village in the mountainous region of China, there lived a girl who was exceptionally clever with her hands. In weaving or embroidery, no one could match her skill. She was pretty, too—as beautiful as the poppy that grows in the fields—and thrifty besides. Her name was Ling-Li.

Opposite Ling-Li's house there lived a boy named Manchang. Ever since they were little, the two children played together. And as the one was known for her thriftiness and skill in homespun crafts and the other for his diligence and skill in farming, the two became close friends. Their parents noticed how well suited they were for each other and, according to ancient custom, arranged their betrothal.

Manchang's parents were very poor. All they could afford to give as a betrothal gift was two baskets of double-eared corn, a large green cabbage, a sheaf of violet peas with striped pods, and two strings of red chili peppers. But to Ling-Li these vegetables were the most beautiful gifts in the world. She carefully placed them where she could look at them first thing in the morning when she awoke and last thing at night before she went to sleep.

Manchang and Ling-Li were to be married in the autumn. Ling-Li's parents wanted to sell everything they could spare in order to buy wedding clothes for their daughter. But Ling-Li would not have it. "I can make my own wedding robe," she said. With money he had saved, Manchang bought Ling-Li several catties of raw cotton, and she set to work.

In the same village there lived a girl called Golden Flower. She, too, was to be married that autumn, to the son of a wealthy family. The groom's parents sent Golden Flower expensive gifts— intricately engraved bracelets of ivory, beautiful brocaded jackets, and dazzlingly embroidered satin robes. Golden Flower tried on this and that. All day long she kept changing her clothes, making up her face, and gazing at her reflection.

All the other girls in the village admired Golden Flower's new clothes, but Ling-Li did not so much as cast a glance at them. She spun the cotton Manchang had given her, wove the thread into cloth, and made it into a wedding robe. Then she embroidered the robe with patterns of the double-eared corn and the green cabbage, the red chili peppers, and the violet peas. The corn looked as if it were made of gold, the cabbage of jade, the chili of red coral, and the violet peas of dragon's gall. The more she embroidered, the more intricate the patterns became, and the more beautiful they looked.

Day after day Ling-Li stitched busily from morning till evening. Sometimes she pricked her finger with the needle and a drop of blood fell onto the robe, and there she would embroider a red flower. Sometimes she became tired and beads of sweat soiled the cloth, and here she would embroider butterflies.

For three whole months she worked, and at last the robe was finished. It was lovelier than the changing clouds in the sky and more colorful than a meadow in full bloom.

On the day the robe was finished, Golden Flower happened to pass by Ling-Li's house. When she saw the robe she was overcome with envy.

"Ling-Li," she said, "I'll give you ten embroidered satin robes and six brocaded jackets for your wedding robe."

"No," Ling-Li replied, "I won't exchange, for nothing can compare with this robe of mine."

But Golden Flower was used to having her way. Before Ling-Li had time to realize what was happening, Golden Flower snatched up the robe and ran out the door. "I'll wear it for a day, then I'll return it to you," she called over her shoulder.

Ling-Li determined to trap the magpies and get back her wedding robe. From the thread she had left over, she wove a large net.

Early the next morning the magpies flew over Ling-Li's house. They perched on the roof and chattered incessantly. As soon as Ling-Li heard them she ran into the garden, spread her net, and threw a handful of grain on it. The magpies flew down to peck at the grain. With a pull of her rope, Ling-Li caught them in the net, but as she drew the net toward her, the magpies suddenly flapped their wings and flew off, lifting the net and Ling-Li into the sky.

Flying at high speed, they soared toward the rising sun. All Ling-Li could hear was the sighing of the wind. The rice fields below her looked like patches of red and green, disappearing into the distance.

The magpies flew on and on until they reached the peak of a high mountain. There they gently set Ling-Li on the ground. All around her were green trees where birds of every kind—larks, golden orioles, peacocks, parrots, and doves— hopped from branch to branch. The magpies tore the net into shreds to free themselves.

As soon as the magpies joined the others, all the birds began to sing. Startled by the sound, Ling-Li looked up and saw a spirit maiden, dressed in a beautifully embroidered robe, approaching her. Ling-Li was puzzled, for the robe was the one that the magpies had taken from her.

The spirit maiden spoke in a kind voice. "Ling-Li, your robe is beautiful, but I have one even more beautiful. Will you exchange?"

"I'm sorry," Ling-Li replied, "but I cannot, for this is my wedding robe that I've made myself."

"Oh," said the spirit maiden, "then I'll return it to you at once." And she took off the robe and gave it back to Ling-Li. "Thank you for letting me wear it. May you and your husband live in harmony and have a rich, full life together." Before Ling-Li could reply, the spirit maiden turned and disappeared.

As Ling-Li stood there, thinking herself in a dream, she saw a dazzlingly colored phoenix fly out of the woods. Immediately, the other birds took wing and followed it.

"It must have been the Phoenix Fairy, the Queen of the Birds," thought Ling-Li. Then, taking her wedding robe, she tripped merrily down the mountain toward home.

Halfway there she met Manchang, beside himself with worry. Early that morning, as he was working in the fields, he had seen the flock of magpies carrying the net with Ling-Li dangling from it. He immediately gave chase, but the birds flew so fast he was soon left behind.

Ling-Li told him everything that had happened. Manchang, in return, told her that the bridal chamber had been cleaned and whitewashed and that all was ready for the wedding.

The next day, dressed in her lovely embroidered wedding robe made with her own hands, Ling-Li became Manchang's bride. And no couple was ever happier.

After the wedding Ling-Li was more industrious and thrifty than ever. At the break of day with the call of the chattering magpies, she would put on her embroidered robe and go out into the fields to work. Whenever she felt too warm, she would take the robe off and carefully lay it on the ground. Then the magpies would appear and circle overhead, on the lookout in case someone should try to steal it.

One day while Ling-Li was helping Manchang with the harvest, she took off her robe and laid it on a ridge. Just at that moment Golden Flower was returning from town to visit her parents. As she walked along the ridge, she saw the embroidered robe lying there. Stealthily she snatched it up and flung it across her shoulders. But as she was thrusting her hands into the sleeves, a flock of magpies swooped down from the sky. With loud caws they encircled the thief and pecked at her. Shielding her face with her hands, Golden Flower ran and hid herself from her persistent pursuers. In all the confusion the embroidered robe was torn to shreds. Golden Flower's face, too, was gashed, and even after her wounds healed her face showed ugly scars.

The varicolored shreds of cloth looked like thousands of beautiful flowers as they danced in the breeze, chased by butterflies. They drifted farther and farther away and then gradually fluttered to the ground, strewn all over the fields and newly upturned soil.

The following spring, clusters of tender plants appeared in the fields. Whenever Ling-Li saw these plants she felt a pang in her heart, for they reminded her of her lost robe. She dug the plants up one by one and planted them in her garden. By summer they were full grown, with reddish-brown stems, shiny green leaves, and blood-red flowers.

To Ling-Li the flowers looked like the colorful phoenix bird with outstretched wings in its flight to the sun.

Afterword

The Chinese phoenix, *feng huang*, is entirely different from the fabled bird in Greek mythology. The ancient Greeks believed that only one phoenix, always male, existed at a time. That mythological bird lived for five hundred years, then burned itself on a funeral pyre. From its ashes there rose a young phoenix, symbolizing immortality.

In Chinese mythology, there is not one phoenix, but two—the male *feng* and the female *huang*. Together they symbolize union. Later, the phoenix came to symbolize the female or *yin* principle, and the dragon, the male or *yang* principle. The phoenix is mentioned in texts dating back to the end of the second millennium B.C.E. Its presence was a sign that the reigning ruler was honorable and just. When the Chinese philosopher Confucius (551?–478? B.C.E.) complained that "the phoenix appears no more," he meant that the government was corrupt and there was no prospect for improvement.

The *feng huang* is described in Chinese literature as a creature six feet high, with a cock's head, a snake's neck, a swallow's beak, and a tortoise's back. However, when ancient Chinese artists depicted the bird, they chose not to follow this description, but to create a magnificent creature that was part peacock, part pheasant, and part bird of paradise. Its feathers were a blending of five colors, red, white, yellow, azure, and black, representing the qualities of virtue, duty, correct behavior, humanity, and reliability. The tail feathers were adorned with "peacock eyes," just as Zong-Zhou Wang has painted them. The two longer middle feathers were especially beautiful, and Zong-Zhou Wang has pictured the phoenix fairy holding them in her hands when she meets Ling-Li. The Chinese phoenix is ruler of the birds and is said to love music. A pair of Chinese phoenixes is a symbol of happiness and good fortune.

The Chinese call the flower that reminded Ling-Li of the phoenix bird in its flight to the sun *Feng Xian Hua* (pronounced like "Fung-Shien Hwah") or "phoenix fairy flower." It is related to a common wildflower in the United States, known as jewelweed.

I wish to express my appreciation to Ai-Ling Louie and to Anna Wang of the Monmouth County (NJ) Public Library; Martin Heijdra of the Gest Oriental Library, Princeton University; Carole Walton of St. Mary's College, Notre Dame; and storyteller Susan Danoff for their assistance with my research. My main printed sources about the *feng huang* were *Chinese Mythology* by Anthony Christie (Hamlyn, 1968), *A Dictionary of Chinese Symbols* by Wolfram Eberhard (Routledge, 1988), and, for children, *Classical Calliope*, Volume V, Number III (Summer 1985), published by Cobblestone Publishing Inc.

Ellin Greene